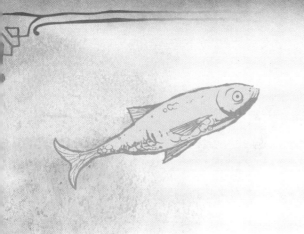

CITY OF
CHEESEBRIDGE

THE BOXTROLLS™

HIGH VOLTAGE

Little, Brown and Company

Hachette Book Group
237 Park Avenue, New York, NY 10017
Visit our website at lb-kids.com

Little, Brown and Company is a division of Hachette Book Group, Inc.
The Little, Brown name and logo are trademarks of Hachette Book Group, Inc.

First Edition: September 2014

ISBN 978-0-316-33265-1

10 9 8 7 6 5 4 3 2 1

CW

Printed in the United States of America

The Stinkiest Cheese
in Cheesebridge

Adapted by Emily C. Hughes
Screenplay by Irena Brignull & Adam Pava
Based upon the book *Here Be Monsters!* by Alan Snow

Little, Brown and Company
New York • Boston

Even though he is allergic, all Mr. Archibald Snatcher has ever wanted is to be part of Cheesebridge's fancy cheese-tasting club, in which members wear big white hats and have long conversations about cheeses rare and wonderful.

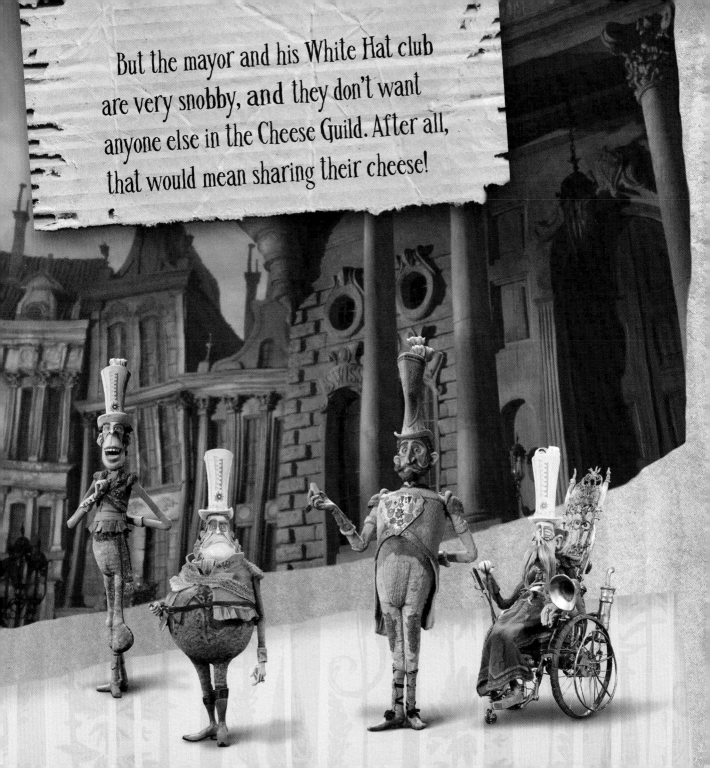

But the mayor and his White Hat club are very snobby, and they don't want anyone else in the Cheese Guild. After all, that would mean sharing their cheese!

The White Hats love cheese above all other things. They can't be bothered with Snatcher's dream, let alone with the creatures he says terrorize their town every night.

And besides, Snatcher isn't very . . . nice.

Snatcher will stop at nothing to get what he wants. He tells the mayor that he'll rid the town of Boxtrolls in exchange for a white hat.

Lord Portley-Rind, sure that Snatcher will
never achieve the goal, agrees to the deal.

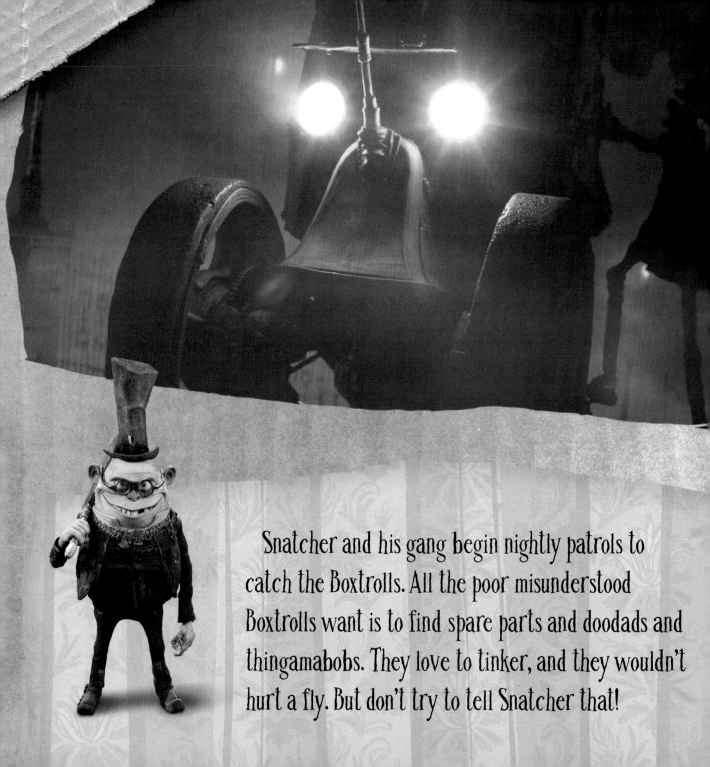

Snatcher and his gang begin nightly patrols to catch the Boxtrolls. All the poor misunderstood Boxtrolls want is to find spare parts and doodads and thingamabobs. They love to tinker, and they wouldn't hurt a fly. But don't try to tell Snatcher that!

The Red Hats have a truck outfitted with all kinds of traps and snares and nets to round up every Boxtroll in sight, and they're good at what they do. They find a lot of Boxtrolls, and a boy named Eggs among them!

While the Red Hats snatch up Boxtrolls left and right, Eggs and his posh friend Winnie hatch a plan. They need to organize a resistance.

They discover that the captured Boxtrolls
are in Snatcher's factory, being held prisoner
and forced to build a mysterious machine.

But before Eggs and Winnie are able to rescue
their friends, Snatcher invades the Boxtrolls' home
and captures the rest of them!

The situation looks hopeless to Eggs,
and Snatcher seems to have won.

Ready to receive his reward, Snatcher takes his prisoners to the Cheese Guild. But when the townsfolk discover that the Boxtrolls are actually friendly, Lord Portley-Rind changes his mind about giving Snatcher a white hat.

Even members of the Red Hats start to have their doubts about their leader.

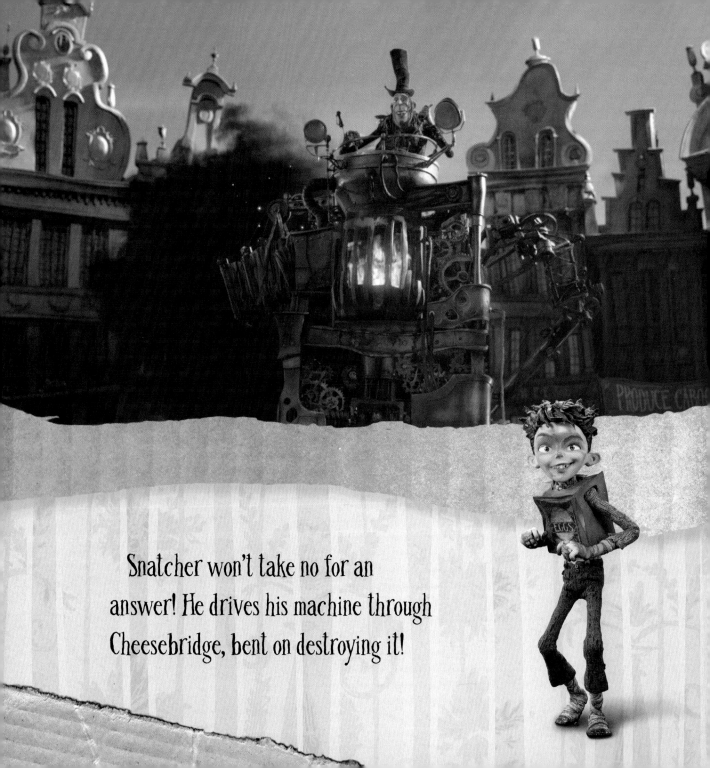

Snatcher won't take no for an answer! He drives his machine through Cheesebridge, bent on destroying it!

With Eggs leading the charge, the Boxtrolls finally stand up for themselves! They defeat Snatcher's monstrous machine. (When you're the one who put something together, taking it apart is easy.) The town is saved from destruction! Until . . .

. . . a runaway wheel of Brie turns
Snatcher into an allergic monster.

He takes Winnie captive and threatens to take control of Cheesebridge once and for all.

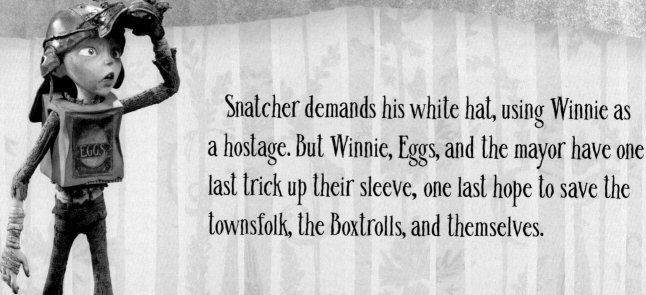

Snatcher demands his white hat, using Winnie as a hostage. But Winnie, Eggs, and the mayor have one last trick up their sleeve, one last hope to save the townsfolk, the Boxtrolls, and themselves.

They invite Snatcher in to taste the
rarest of cheeses. . . .

Can Snatcher be defeated by the stinkiest cheese in Cheesebridge?